# Learn With Me Presents:

## A guide to strategic reading

**Written by:**

**Jessica Collett**

**Craig Collett**

*Limited permission granted to reproduce this book*

*Read With Me:* A Guide to Strategic Reading
*Learn with Me*
Written by Jessica Collett and Craig Collett
Layout and Cover Design by Craig Collett
Edited by Craig Collett

© Copyright 2010 Learn with Me, LLC
All rights reserved.

Reprint Permissions, Learn With Me
P.O. Box 58
Meridian, ID 83680

Printed in the United States of America
ISBN 978-1-4507-0588-2

# Table of Contents

# Introduction

**What is *Read With Me*?**

*Read With Me* is designed to assist home educators and teachers in giving students a positive experience with literature each and every time they open a book. Books have a unique way of connecting us with values and building character. However, this doesn't simply occur just from reading words on a page. One must consciously search for these connections and apply them into the way he or she lives. *Read With Me* is a resource for any language arts educator that includes:

- Reading strategies
- How to annotate a text
- Questions to apply to any work of literature
- Pre-reading activities
- Activities while reading
- Post-reading activities
- Vocabulary ideas
- Definitions and examples of 100 important literary terms

**What is strategic reading?**

In 1780, Abigail Adams stated, "Learning is not attained by chance; it must be sought for with ardor and attended to with diligence." Strategic reading can be viewed the same way. It is implementing the proper tools necessary to comprehend individual pieces of literature. This takes "ardor" and "diligence." Reading strategically is the groundwork for drawing values from literature and learning the lessons supplied there.

**Do Something!**

We believe that it's not enough to just read, but that a reader must *do something* with what they are reading. Truly connecting with literature takes effort, and students make these connections in a variety of ways (kinesthetically, visually, linguistically, etc). Thinking about the work is just the beginning of the learning process. *Read With Me* provides various activities and ideas to help a person do something beyond just reading a book. When you do something in addition to reading, you have an opportunity to synthesize information and thus, learn.

We hope that the ideas in *Read with Me* will ignite a love of reading and ultimately a love of learning.

# What are strategies?  Tools for success!

Reading strategies are methods used while reading that increase retention, connect the reader with themes, increase comprehension, and ultimately enhance learning.  You can view strategies like tools in a tool box (Dean 1).  Just as certain problems require a hammer or a wrench, certain texts require different approaches or methods.

The following strategies are tools that all good readers apply.  Some readers naturally visualize what they are reading, while others need to consciously make an effort to picture what is being said.  Others cannot help but guess what is going to happen next in a story *(predict),* while some might not find themselves as engaged. The next time you read something, take the time to survey which strategies you naturally employ and make a list of what methods you need to practice.

# Reading Strategies

**Visualize:** Can you visualize the landscape described in the opening section of the passage?  What do you think the character looks like?  Skilled readers learn how to form a mental picture in their heads as if the story is playing like a movie.  Readers can also visualize the events and characters of the story by using the descriptions given in the work to draw a picture.  Learning how to visualize is one of the keys to improving reading comprehension.

**Summarize:** Summarize what has been read in your own words.  What is the story about?  What is the central conflict?  What is the main idea?  If you cannot summarize the section that you just read, go back and try it again.  It is important to stop periodically and summarize a section (line, paragraph, page, or chapter) to show that you understand what the author was trying to say.  Summaries can be done by drawing pictures, telling another person about the passage, acting out a scene, or writing a paragraph.

**Question:** Ask questions that invite discussion and thought throughout the work.  Questioning causes one to analyze the material and gives an opportunity dig deeper into themes and important concepts. Question the actions of characters or the choices of the author.  One might ask "Did Romeo *really* love Rosaline if he was able to move on so quickly"?  This question might lead to a discussion about the theme of love and what it means to truly love another person.  Some great questions are "why" questions.  For example: why do you think the author chose to name the book *The Giver?* Another thought-provoking question to ask is "what is the significance or purpose of … "?

**Clarify:** If you do not understand something, STOP!  Take the time to clarify any parts that were unclear. Look up words that are new to you and reread the passage with your new understanding.

**Infer:** To infer means to come to a conclusion by gathering evidence or making an educated guess. Good readers make inferences about characters and what will happen next in the story as they read. For example, look at the cover of a book. Based on the title (and the illustration), what can you infer the book is going to be about? You can begin making inferences before you even open the book—and you should!

**Predict:** What do you think will happen next in the story? Was your prediction correct? As you read to discover if you accurately forecasted the fate of a character, you will be much more engaged. It might be fun to write down your predictions and record the actual outcome to see if you were correct.

**Connect:** One of the best things you can do to make a book seem more real is to try to make connections to the story. As you read, try to connect with things you have seen or read before; this will make the text more meaningful. For example, have you ever felt misunderstood? If you have, then you can relate (*connect)* to Anne Frank. Does a character remind you of a song you have heard? Does a movie remind you of book you read? The more associations you can make with the story, the more alive and realistic the characters will become in your mind.

> **Connection question**: "Of what does this remind me?"

**Reflect:** After completing a work, it is important to take the time to reflect about what you have read. Reflection can be done in the form of discussion, journal entries, essays, art projects, and so on. This allows you to synthesize the information and gives time to make connections to the work.

> **Reflective Reading**:
>
> After reading, finish these sentences
>   1. I learned
>   2. I was surprised
>   3. I wonder
>   4. I feel
>   5. I enjoyed

**Remember:** Reading strategically ultimately means you are reading to succeed. It might slow down your reading at first to stop and clarify, but in the end you will be able to incorporate these strategies without even thinking about it; ultimately, your comprehension will improve and so will your ability to retain what was read.

# Annotating Texts: Having a Conversation With the Work

When you read, make sure you are armed with the proper tools to succeed: a pencil, a study journal, and a dictionary.

One of the most common complaints about annotating is that it slows down the reading process. That is the point! Slow down so you can really process the information. By taking the time to underline, question, predict, etc, as you read, you understand the text on a much deeper level!

If you annotate texts as you read, you cannot help but pay attention to what you are reading. Also, it will be easier to find the important information if it is marked. Once you get in the habit of annotating, reading will become a much more meaningful and memorable experience.

**How do I annotate?**

View the text as if it were a person talking to you. If you are confused, stop and write a question in the margins about what confuses you. If you passionately agree with a statement (or disagree), tell the author how you feel by writing your opinion next to the passage. If there is not enough room to write your thoughts, you can get a package of sticky notes on which to annotate.

The important thing is to find a style and a system that works for you. Don't be afraid to try different methods. Here are some ideas about how to annotate:

- **Make brief comments in the margins**. Use any white space that is available (the inside cover, the title page, etc). Write your questions and comments wherever there is space.

- **Underline important quotes**. If the passage is long, just put brackets around the beginning and the end. Write in the margins why that particular passage stood out to you.

- **Mark new vocabulary**. Putting a box around new words is a great method to mark vocabulary; other people enjoy circling or drawing clouds around new words. It might be helpful to write the definition of the word in the margins.

- **Name the chapter**. If a chapter is unnamed, take the liberty of naming it. If it is named, write whether or not you would have named the chapter something different.

- **Make connections**. If there are words, phrases, or ideas that connect, draw an arrow to physically connect the two ideas. If a particular part reminds you of something, make note of it next to the passage

- **Use symbols**. Come up with a system of symbols (triangles, stars, circles, etc.) and abbreviations to mark different things; you can create a legend on the title page to help you remember your code.

**What do I annotate?**

In a nutshell, annotate anything that pops out at you. If you think it is important, make a comment or draw a symbol. When you annotate, you are simply taking notes in the book while you read.

**Make note of the following things:**

- Anything that you would like to discuss or did not understand

- The mood and tone of the work

- The point of view of the narrator

- The repetition of ides, words, phrases, actions or events

- The effect of word choices and writing strategies

- Key events

- Imagery and figurative language

- Metaphors, similes and allusions*

- Irony and any other literary devices

*See *Important Literary Terms* section for definitions.

## Comment about the following things:

- The actions or development of characters – especially how characters change throughout the work

- Anything that makes you surprised, angry, excited, intrigued, disturbed, etc.

- Connections to other works

- Passages that are powerful or meaningful

- Lessons you learn from the work

- Themes

Annotating gives you the opportunity to consciously practice reading strategically. Remember, visualize, summarize, question, clarify, infer, predict, connect and reflect as you read!

# 20 Universal Questions to apply to any work

These questions can be used in a variety of ways.  They're great for checking comprehension, essay prompts, deep thinking, test questions, and making connections with the work.  These are questions that strategic readers constantly answer in their minds as they read.  They provide purpose for reading a work of literature and are a springboard for analysis.

1.  What is the significance of the title?  (What information can you infer from the title?)
2.  What was the historical context in which the work was written?
3.  What was the author's purpose in writing the work?
4.  What is the setting of the story?
5.  What is the mood of the story?
6.  How does the setting affect the mood?
7.  Who is the protagonist?  Describe the protagonist's characteristics.
8.  Who is the antagonist?  Describe the antagonist's characteristics.
9.  What is the central conflict?  How is it resolved?
10. From what point of view is the story written?
11. How might the story be different if it were written from a different character's point of view?
12. Is there any symbolism in the story?  If so, list the symbols and what they represent.
13. Does the protagonist change throughout the story?  If so, how?  What causes this change?
14. Do you admire any of the characters?  Why or why not?
15. What are the three most important quotes in the story?  What insight about characters do these quotes give?
16. Do you think the ending is appropriate for the story?  Why or why not?
17. What lessons can be learned from this work?
18. What are the themes of the work?
19. Of what does this work remind you?
20. Did this book change your perspective about anything?  If so, how?

An easy way to remember these questions is to use a bookmark like the one below while you read.

## Identify the Following:

Significance of the title:

Historical context:

Author's purpose:

Setting:

Mood:

Protagonist:

Antagonist:

Central conflict:

Point of view:

Symbolism:

Themes:

Three most important quotes:

Lessons from the work:

This reminds me of …

# Pre-Reading Activities

The following activities are designed to activate prior knowledge and build background information about the work being studied. It is important to understand the historical context of any work, as this knowledge will add great insight to the story. These ideas can be used before reading or implemented throughout the reading process.

# ABC Research Chart:

**Objectives:**
- To build background knowledge about the topic
- To make connections between historical events and the story

**Directions:**
- Pick a topic pertaining to the work and research it.
- Write one fact for every letter of the alphabet next to the letter. The fact can start with the letter or be the subject of the sentence.

A

B

C

D

E

F

G

H

I

J

K

L

M

N

O

P

Q

R

S

T

U

V

W

X

Y

Z

(Antinarella)

# KWL

## Objectives:

- To activate prior knowledge
- To create an interest in learning
- To keep a record of what is learned

## Directions:

- Record the information that you already know about the topic under the "What I *K*now" column.
- Write what specific facts you would like to learn through researching in the "What I *W*ant to learn" column.
- After reading the work, record what you have learned in the "What I *L*earned" column.

| What I *K*now | What I *W*ant to learn | What I *L*earned |
|---|---|---|
|  |  |  |

(Ogle 626)

# Design a Stamp

**Objectives:**

- To activate prior knowledge
- To build background information about the subject
- To understand the historical context of the story

**Directions:**

- Research the time period in which the work takes place.
- Select an image that accurately symbolizes the time period. Design a stamp that could represent that era.
- Write a letter to the Citizen's Stamp Advisory Committee (the committee that decides stamp designs) defending why your stamp should be chosen to represent that decade or time period.

**Example:** If you were going to read *The Great Gatsby* by F. Scott Fitzgerald, it would be helpful to research the 1920's to understand the culture and the story. Below is a sample design of a stamp that represents the 1920's. (Stamp designed by Madisen Miller.)

(Dean 128)

# Write a report

**Objectives:**

- To build background knowledge
- To improve comprehension of the story

**Directions:**

- Research a topic pertaining to the work.
- Take notes on your research.
- Write a formal research report on your findings.
- Teach the main points of your report to another person.

**Example:** If you are reading *The Devil's Arithmetic* by Jane Yolen, it would greatly enhance your understanding of the time period to do a report on a particular concentration camp.

**Option:** Create a Power-point (or other type of multi-media) presentation to enhance your lesson.

Note: Research can be done before or after reading the work.

# Seven Statements

**Objectives:**

- To build background knowledge about the topic
- To form opinions about the text
- To explore and understand themes from the work

**Directions:**

- Write seven statements about the themes and the historical context of the book.
- Mark whether you agree or disagree with the statement and justify your answer in the space provided.
- After you have read the work, review your answers and see if your opinion has changed.

| Statement | Agree? | Disagree? | Why? |
|---|---|---|---|
|  |  |  |  |
|  |  |  |  |
|  |  |  |  |
|  |  |  |  |
|  |  |  |  |
|  |  |  |  |
|  |  |  |  |

**Example**: Four themes in George Orwell's novel *1984* are power, government, war and peace. The following statements reflect these themes.

| Statement | Agree? | Disagree? | Why? |
|---|---|---|---|
| Knowledge is power. | | | |
| Absolute power corrupts absolutely. | | | |
| Peace is the absence of war. | | | |
| The only people with power are those in the government. | | | |
| History never repeats itself. | | | |
| Accounts of history are recorded accurately and without bias. | | | |
| The government has the right to monitor those who are considered "dangerous". | | | |

# Prediction Journal

**Objectives:**

- To build anticipation and interest in the text
- To create a focus and purpose for reading

**Directions:**

- Make a prediction for each section of the work and record it in the space provided.
- Record the actual outcome of your prediction in the space next to your written prediction.

| Prediction | Actual Outcome |
|---|---|
|  |  |
|  |  |
|  |  |
|  |  |
|  |  |

# Cultural Connection

**Objectives:**

- To build background knowledge about the topic
- To understand the historical context of the story
- To create cultural relevance

**Directions:**

- Listen to music from the time period in which the work is set.
- Write a one page response describing what you learned about the culture and the time period after listening to the music.

Examine the following elements while listening to the music to guide your response:
1. Lyrics (if any)
2. Rhythm
3. Beat
4. Tempo
5. Choice of instruments
6. Style
7. Dynamics

*What specifically can you infer about the lifestyle, values, and culture of the time period?

**Example:** If you are going to read *The Great Gatsby,* listen to jazz and swing music that was composed in the 1920's. Record what you learned about the culture and values of the roaring 20's from listening to the music.

**Variation:** Learn a dance from the time period. Record what you learned about the time period from this experience in a one page response.

**Example:** If you are going to read *The Great Gatsby,* learn the Charleston.

# Diorama

**Objectives:**

- To comprehend an element of the work at a deeper level
- To improve comprehension of the text
- To make connections with the story

**Directions:**

- Create a diorama of something that played an important role in the story.
- Use the facts and descriptions from the work to help you create your project.
- Draw a sketch of your diorama before you actually create it. Make sure you figure out the dimensions of the structure.
- Come up with a plan detailing what materials you will use.

**Example:** If you are reading *The Diary of a Young Girl* by Anne Frank, you could make a diorama of the secret annex that Frank and the van Daan families lived in while in hiding. This could be constructed out of a variety of materials: a cardboard box, building blocks, construction paper, coat hangers, or even macaroni noodles. Be creative!

# Characterization Activities

These activities are created to help the reader analyze and evaluate the characters in the novel. Understanding how characters develop throughout a story leads to a greater comprehension of the work as a whole. Also, studying characters is a great way to extract theme as well as infer the author's purpose in writing (as authors often use characters as a mouthpiece for their own ideas). Please note that these activities can be done while reading the story or after you have completed the work.

# Who is who in the story?
# Make a Bookmark of the Characters

**Objectives:**

- To increase understanding of the characters in the work
- To improve comprehension of the story

**Directions:**

- Make a bookmark listing all of the characters in the work.
- Write a brief description of each of the characters. As you learn more about the character throughout the work, add to the description.

**Example:** Make a bookmark listing all of the characters in *Romeo and Juliet.* In the story, there are two households that are in a feud. Place all of the people of the house of Montague on one side, and the people of the Capulet household on the other side. Designate a side on which to write the other characters (neutral).

**Option:** Draw a picture of the character (this can be done in place of the written description or in addition to it.)

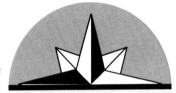

*The Capulets*
   **Lord Capulet**: Juliet's father; enemy of Lord Montague
   **Lady Capulet:** Juliet's mother
   **Juliet:** The 13 year-old daughter of Lord and Lady Capulet
   **Tybalt:** Nephew to Lady Capulet
   **Nurse:** Juliet's former nursemaid
   **Peter:** The Nurse's servant
   **Sampson:** Capulet's servant
   **Gregory**: Capulet's servant

*Others*
   **Friar John:** Priest from Mantua
   **County Paris:** A young count; kinsman to the Prince
   **Apothecary:** A 14th century pharmacist

*The Montagues*
   **Lord Montague**: Romeo's father; enemy of Lord Capulet
   **Lady Montague:** Romeo's mother
   **Romeo:** The14 year-old son of Lord and Lady Montague
   **Benvolio:** Romeo's cousin and friend
   **Balthasar:** Romeo's servant
   **Abraham:** Montague's servant

*Others*
   **Prince Escalus:** The ruler of Verona
   **Mercutio:** Kinsman to the Prince and Romeo's friend
   **Friar Laurence:** Priest from Verona

# Motto

**Objectives:**

- To analyze and evaluate the characters
- To increase understanding of the characters
- To explore and analyze themes of the work

**Directions:**

- Pick a character from the work to analyze.
- Write a motto that describes the character's philosophies or views about life.
- Make a poster, banner, or badge to display the character's motto.

> **Motto:** A catchword, phrase or sentence that describes a person or institution's beliefs.

**Helpful Hint:** Pick a quote from the story that describes the character's beliefs; or, find a scene that illustrates the character's values and summarize it in a phrase or a sentence.

**Examples:** A famous motto from Star Wars is said by the Jedi master, "Do, or do not. There is no try." A motto from Shakespeare's *Hamlet* could be summarized by the advice given to Laertes from Polonius: "This above all else: To thine own self be true."

Atticus Finch, a character from Harper Lee's novel *To Kill a Mockingbird* told his children that "you never really understand a person until you consider things from his point of view . . . until you climb into his skin and walk around in it."

**Here are two mottos that summarize Atticus' ideology:**
Try on someone else's shoes!
Change your perspective!

*Writing a character's motto is a good activity to help readers infer themes, as the motto might also be a theme of the story.

# Character Sketch and Analysis

**Objectives:**

- To increase understanding of the characters in the work
- To improve comprehension of the story
- To analyze and discuss the characters

**Directions:**

- Pick a character from the work and draw it. This can be done on a regular-sized piece of paper or on a poster.
- List the character's five most dominant qualities and attributes on the picture.
- Find a quote from the work illustrating each of the attributes that you listed and write the quote underneath the attribute.

**Example:** *Tuesdays With Morrie* by Mitch Albom is about an old professor named Morrie Schwartz who is dying of ALS. In his last stage of life, Morrie did what he knew how to do best: he taught. This time, the course was on how to live. Morrie's illness and imminent death gave him a new perspective on life, and he chose to share that with others.

Trait number 1: Optimistic

The following quote from the novel demonstrates Morrie's optimism even in the face of adversity:

"I may be dying, but I am surround by loving, caring souls. How many people can say that?"

# Character Description

**Objectives:**
- To increase understanding of the characters in the work
- To improve comprehension of the story
- To analyze the characters

**Directions:**
- Pick a character from the work to analyze.
- Use the chart to list the character's physical and personality traits.
- Draw a picture of the character in the space provided.

Character's name: _____ Age: _____ Role in story: _____

| Physical Traits | Personality Traits |
|---|---|
|  |  |

**Draw a picture of the character**

# Resume

**Objectives:**

- To analyze a character in the work
- To understand the story at a deeper level
- To learn how to create a resume and a cover letter
- To learn about a career and the application process

**Directions:**

- Pick a main character from the work that is well-developed.
- If your character were to apply for a job, what job do you think he/she would be well qualified for?
- Make a list of traits the character has that makes him/her qualified for the position your picked.
- Create a resume for the character describing how that character is qualified for the job you selected.
- Create a cover letter.

**Example:** Odysseus, the protagonist in Homer's epic poem, *The Odyssey,* is a skilled soldier with years of experience in fighting wars. If he needed a job, Odysseus would make a fantastic police officer or be a great addition to the CIA.

**Variation:** Find a real job application for the field you chose and fill it out as if you were the character. If you thought that Odysseus should become a police officer, acquire a real application from a police department and fill it out as if you were Odysseus.

    * Before you create your resume and cover letter, find an example that teaches the correct format.

# Letter of Advice

## Objectives:

- To analyze the conflict in the story
- To evaluate a character's choices and moral code
- To help the reader make connections with the text

## Directions:

- Write a letter from the perspective of a character in the story asking for advice about a problem that needs to be solved.
- Answers the character's letter by giving advice as to how to solve the problem. Make sure that the facts in your letter are consistent with the story and that your advice is realistic. Justify your advice.

**Option:** Write a letter in the form of an advice column

**Example:** This is a letter written to an advice columnist from Juliet after she has just heard the news of Romeo's banishment (The end of Act III from *Romeo and Juliet).*

Dear Abby,

I need your help! My parents have arranged for me to marry a man named Paris on Thursday. The problem is – I do not love him. I am in love my father's sworn enemy Romeo (doesn't his name just sound romantic?). Romeo and I were secretly wed by Friar Lawrence earlier this week To make matters worse, my new husband slew my cousin Tybalt while trying to defend his friend Mercutio in a fray. My dear beloved Romeo has now been banished from Verona by the Prince. I do not want to disappoint my parents, but I do not want to be with a man whom I do not love. What should I do?

From, betrothed but already wed

Dear betrothed but already wed,

It sounds like you are tangled in a sticky web of love and hatred. From your letter, I would guess that you have much of your life to still live. Please keep in mind that the choices you make now will affect the way you spend the rest of your life. Do not decide anything too hastily, as a wise friar once said "Wisely and slow, they stumble that run fast." You need to take the time to weigh out your options and the subsequent results. Consider what is most important in your life and make your decision based on what you value the highest. Good luck!

# Change Perspective

**Objectives:**

- To analyze an important scene from the story
- To help the reader connect with the text
- To improve comprehension of the story

**Directions:**

- Pick a scene or chapter from the work and rewrite it from a different character's perspective. By writing the same event from a new perspective, you will understand the story and the different characters in a new way.

**Example:** *The Adventures of Huckleberry Finn* is told from the perspective of a young, uneducated, teen-aged boy named Huckleberry Finn. At the beginning of the story, he lives with Widow Douglas. Here is how the story might have sounded if she had been narrating the story when Huck was kidnapped by his drunken father (written by Julia Henrie).

Last night Huck never came home. Dinner was so quiet without his rather obnoxious behavior. Weeks went by and Huck had still not come home. Then one day I found out that Huck's dad had taken him to some shabby cabin a couple of miles down the river, so I sent a gentleman to go check on Huck, but Pop rudely turned the man away and threatened him and anyone who ever tried to come to the cabin again. I was coming to realize how much I really did miss Huck, even though he wasn't the most civilized boy I have ever met in my life.

Then the news came of Huck's murder! I didn't know what to feel, but I did know one thing and that was that I would find Huck's body and give him a proper burial. We looked and looked for his body but we never found it.

This gave me hope that maybe somewhere Huck is okay and is living a much better life than what he was with Pap, but who am I kidding, that kind of stuff only happens in fairy tales. I guess it does not hurt to hope, but I know that Huck went to the good place—even though he was a bit rough on the edges, he had a good heart that was the size of Texas.

# During Activities

These activities are helpful strategies to apply while reading a work. They help organize information and provide purpose in reading. Ultimately, these activities will help improve comprehension of the work.

# Summarize the Story

**Objectives:**

- To increase understanding of the work
- To improve comprehension of the story

**Directions:**

- On the left side of the chart, write a summary of the work.
- On the right side of the chart, summarize the work through pictures.

| Written summary | Picture summary |
| --- | --- |
|  |  |

# Quote Journal

**Objectives:**

- To keep a record of important quotes
- To note repeated ideas and thematic elements
- To improve comprehension of the story

**Directions:**

- As you read, write down the quotes that you think are important; use the chart below or your own paper.
- In addition to writing the quote, record the character who said it, the context in which it was spoken, and the page number. If a particular phrase is used more than once or if the title of the work is mentioned, make sure that you write it down!
- After finishing the work, read all of the quotes you have recorded. Use the quotes to analyze characters and infer themes.

| Quote | Character | Context of quote | Page # |
|-------|-----------|------------------|--------|
|       |           |                  |        |
|       |           |                  |        |
|       |           |                  |        |
|       |           |                  |        |
|       |           |                  |        |
|       |           |                  |        |

# Name the Chapters

**Objectives:**

- To analyze the contents of each section
- To improve comprehension of the story
- To help the reader make connections with the text

**Directions:**

- Assign a name for each section or chapter of the work that appropriately describes and summarizes that section.

**If the chapter is already named, answer the following questions about the title:**

1. What is the significance of that section's title?
2. Why do you think the author chose to give the title that name?
3. Do you think the name is a good representation of the section? Justify your answer.
4. If you were to give the section a different name, what would it be? Why?

**If the chapter is unnamed, answer the following questions after assigning it a name:**

1. What is the significance of that section's title?
2. Why did you choose to give the title that name?

# Says/Does

**Objectives:**

- To understand the content of a particular section
- To understand the author's purpose in writing and how that purpose is accomplished.
- To help the reader make connections with the text

**Directions:**

- Read a section of the book and answer the following questions about each section.
- On the left side of the graphic organizer below, summarize the passage. In other words, what is it saying?
- In the middle of the chart, write the section's purpose. What does the author do to accomplish this purpose? What strategy or literary device does the author employ?
- On the right side of the chart, record when you could use that strategy or device in your own writing.

| Says | Does | Future application |
|---|---|---|
|  |  |  |
|  |  |  |
|  |  |  |
|  |  |  |
|  |  |  |

# Venn Diagram

**Objectives:**

- To understand the content of a particular section
- To understand the author's purpose in writing and how that purpose is accomplished.
- To help the reader make connections with the text

**Directions:**

- Pick two characters from the work to compare and contrast.
- Designate a side of the chart for each of the characters.
- On the left side of the chart below, list the characteristics that are unique to character "A" and write the characteristics that are unique to character "B" on the right.
- Write the traits that both characters have in common in the center.

**Variation:** This diagram can be used to compare any element in the work (testimonies, events, etc).

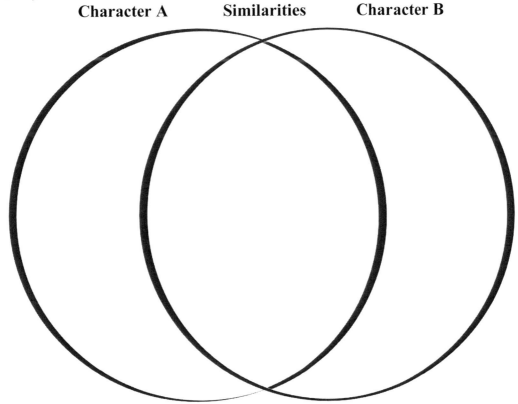

**Character A**         **Similarities**         **Character B**

# Post-Reading Activities

After reading a work, it is imperative to take the time to process and analyze the information; in other words, you need to do something beyond just reading a book! The following activities will help you synthesize the themes and increase your understanding of the work as a whole.

# Newspaper

**Objectives:**

- To understand the historical context of the work
- To learn about the style of writing found in newspapers
- To help the reader connect with the text
- To improve comprehension of the story

**Directions:**

- Make a list of the main events in the work.
- Write a newspaper article featuring each of the events you listed. Give the article a headline that would capture the reader's attention.
- Research the time period and feature articles about historical events that would have made the news.
- Before you write, read an issue of a current paper for ideas on format, style, voice, and layout. Note the type of language and word choices used in newspaper writing; also note how the style changes within the various sections of the paper.
- Come up with a creative name for your paper.

**Options:** A newspaper features many different sections and types of articles. Here are some additional sections you could include in your newspaper:

- Advice column
- Obituaries
- Editorials
- Comics
- Wedding announcements
- Crossword puzzles (using vocabulary words)
- Advertisements*
- Recipes*

This is a big project and can be done by an individual or divided amongst a group.

*You might need to do some research to find out what people ate during this time period or what technology would have been advertised.

# Act out a scene

**Objectives:**

- To analyze an important scene from the story
- To help the reader connect with the text
- To improve comprehension of the story

**Directions:**

- Pick a scene or chapter from the work that played an important part in the plot.*. Turn the scene into a play by writing out the dialect in script form. As you do this, try to capture the voice of the characters.
- Act out the scene for a live audience. It may be helpful to memorize your lines.

*If the scene selected is from a play, memorize the parts and act them out.

**Option:** Make costumes and scenery to perform the play. Or, build a diorama and create little figurines (sock puppets work well too) to act out your scene. You may also video tape your scene.

# Put a character on trial

**Objectives:**

- To analyze a character in-depth
- To dig deeply into the literature and extract new meaning
- To help the reader connect with the text
- To improve comprehension of the story

**Directions:**

- Pick a character from the work who made choices that can be analyzed from different perspectives.
- Put the character "on trial" for a choice he or she made.
- Write opening statements and arguments for prosecuting and defense lawyers.
- Group adaptation: Assign members of your group different parts to play in the trial. You could assign lawyers, a judge, witnesses (different characters from the work) and even a jury. Make sure that all testimonies stay true to the story as written. Use direct quotes and facts from the work for evidence and clues as to what witnesses might say.

**Example:** Put Abigail Williams from Arthur Miller's play *The Crucible* on trial. Was she really guilty of witchcraft? Was she responsible for the hanging of 19 people? Make sure that you use evidence and direct quotes from the play in your testimonies.

# Create a Board Game

**Objectives:**

- To analyze the characters
- To review the contents and key elements of the work
- To improve comprehension of the story
- To help the reader connect with the text

**Directions:**

- Create a board game based on the work. You can model your game after a game that already exists, or create your own game.

**Use the following guidelines to create your game:**

1. Establish rules for your game and write them down.
2. Use the settings from the story as the settings of your game.
3. Incorporate the characters from the story as the game pieces.
4. Compose cards that ask questions about the story.

**Possible card topics**

- Key quotes
- Character
- Setting
- Literary Terms
- Important events or plot questions
- Why questions

(Game created by Parker Yeakley)

# Vote with your feet

**Objectives:**

- To analyze and evaluate the work
- To understand the characters and their choices
- To help the reader connect with the text

**Directions:**

- Pick a topic from the story that could be debated. Write a central question that needs to be answered.
- Debate the topic.

**Example:** The word "scrooge" has become a term used in modern language to describe someone who is miserly or overly stingy, based on the character in *A Christmas Carol* by Charles Dickens. Some believe that Ebenezer Scrooge really behaved like a "scrooge" and that the title is fitting, while others argue that his actions prove otherwise.

On two separate pieces of paper, write the following:

# Ebenezer Scrooge was indeed a "scrooge".

# Ebenezer Scrooge was not a "scrooge".

Place the two pieces of paper on opposite sides of the room and physically "vote with your feet" by standing on the side you agree.

If you are not in a group, you can try to debate both sides with a parent or write an argument for the side of your choice.

# Rewrite the Ending

**Objectives:**

- To analyze and evaluate the ending of the work
- To understand the author's style
- To help the reader connect with the text

**Directions:**

- Pick a point in the plot that would change the outcome of the story if the events had been different. Continue the story from that point to create a new ending.
- As you write, try to be consistent with the established characters. Also try to maintain the author's voice.

**Examples:** In Charlotte Bronte's novel, *Jane Eyre*, some wish that Jane had chosen not to marry Rochester. How would the story have been different if she had chosen another path?

In Shakespeare's tragedy, *Romeo and Juliet,* what would have happened if Romeo had not poisoned himself? How would the story end?

**Option:** Instead of rewriting the ending, continue the story.

# Design a Cover for the Book

**Objectives:**

- To analyze the work as a whole
- To visually represent an important part of the work
- To improve comprehension of the story

**Directions:**

- Think of an image or a scene that could represent the work as a whole.
- Design a cover that could be used for the front of the book.
- Write a paragraph describing how your cover appropriately represents the work.

**Example:** The following picture is of a cover design for Elie Wiesel's book *Night* by Christina Schoppe.

# Adapt a Song

## Objectives:

- To help the reader connect with the text
- To improve comprehension of the story

## Directions:

- Pick a song that you enjoy singing. It is best if you have access to a copy of the lyrics.
- Summarize the main events in the work; or, write a description of a character and how that character changed throughout the story.
- Change the words of the song to summarize the story or highlight a character's experiences.
- Perform your song for another person.

**Example:** Change the words from the song "Old MacDonald Had a Farm" to summarize the events in Orson Scott Card's novel *Ender's Game.*

**Option:** Make a music video of your song. Find costumes and props to retell the story. If you cannot find any costumes, create your own!

# Make a Soundtrack

**Objectives:**

- To make connections with characters in the story
- To help bring the work to life
- To improve comprehension of the story

**Directions:**

- Pick a character in a work and write a brief description about him/her.
- Select music that represents how that character felt throughout the story.
- Make a list of emotions that were felt by different characters throughout the work.
- Select music that portrays that emotion.
- Write a paragraph justifying how your soundtrack accurately portrays the emotions of the work and represents the characters.

**Example:** Imagine you are hired to be on the crew to turn *Island of the Blue Dolphins* by Scott O'Dell into a motion-picture . Your job is to create a soundtrack representing the emotions of the work. Pick a theme song to represent each of the main characters.

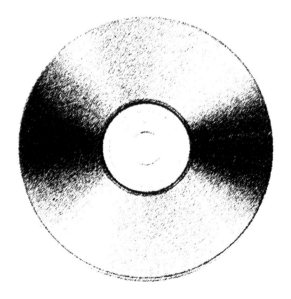

# Make a Brochure

**Objectives:**

- To analyze a particular aspect of the work
- To improve comprehension of the story
- To help the reader connect with the text

**Directions:**

- Create a brochure about the work.

**Brochure ideas:**

- A brochure advertising the work
- A brochure highlighting the literary elements and themes
- A brochure depicting characters and how they changed throughout the work
- A travel brochure of the places visited
- A brochure summarizing the work or a particular section of the story

**Example:** This brochure summarizes Odysseus' encounter with the Cyclops in *The Odyssey* by Homer (brochure created by Samantha Welker).

# Themes

The following activities are designed specifically to help extract the themes and analyze the purpose of the work. These activities are can be done anytime throughout the reading process.

## What is a theme?

A *theme* is the main idea or underlying meaning of a work. It is an idea that has been repeated throughout the work and is often the author's purpose in writing. Sometimes the theme can be extracted from a particular quote; other times the theme can be determined while reflecting about the work as a whole.

As you read, watch for things that are REPEATED. If the author has purposefully included an idea more than once, it is because that idea is important and he or she is trying to place emphasis on it.

### Theme clues:

- Title
- Repeating patterns and symbols
- Allusions to other works
- Repeated quotes or ideas

### Theme questions:

- What did each character learn throughout the work?
- What is the most important scene of the work? Why?
- What is the most important sentence or passage?

### Common themes:

- Good verses evil
- The effects of war
- Coming of age
- Childhood innocence
- Forgiveness
- Intolerance
- Responsibility
- Overcoming challenges
- Remembering the past
- Survival
- Courage

# Synecdoche: Find the theme

**Objectives:**

- To identify and analyze the themes of the work
- To evaluate the author's purpose in writing the novel
- To improve comprehension of the story

**Directions:**

- Identify the MOST IMPORTANT sentence or passage of the entire work (one that could be used to represent the author's message or purpose).
- In a paragraph, write why you picked that particular passage to represent the entire work and why it is the most important part. Also include how this passage embodies a theme of the work.

> The word *synecdoche* has a few meanings; in this case, it is a figure of speech in which a part is used to represent the whole.

**Example:** In the end of her diary, Anne Frank wrote, "I don't think of all the misery, but of the beauty that still remains." This sentence represents her diary as a whole because despite all of the hardships that Anne endured, she still remained optimistic. Anne was able to look past all the hate, death and destruction of the War and trust in a higher power. This unyielding faith demonstrates the themes of optimism, hope and the triumph of the human spirit even in the most challenging circumstances.

# Interview Characters

**Objectives:**

- To understand the characters in the work
- To make connections with the text
- To improve comprehension of the story

**Directions:**

- Imagine that you are a reporter for a local newspaper and that you have been given the assignment to feature some of the characters in the work in an upcoming edition.
- Pick two (or more) characters to "interview" about the lessons they learned from their experiences in the story.
- Write a list of questions to ask your characters.
- Using quotes from the story and your knowledge of the work, answer the questions as if you were the characters.
- Write the articles in the newspaper highlighting the lessons the characters learned.
- After evaluating the lessons learned, make a list of themes of the work.

**Option:** Film your interview and turn it into a news broadcast.

# Theme Cards

**Objectives:**

- To identify and analyze the themes of the work
- To improve comprehension of the story

**Directions:**

- Make a list of themes in the work and write each on a 3x5 card.
- On the other side of the card, describe a scene from the story or find a quote that illustrates each theme.

**Example:** Alan Paton's powerful novel *Cry, the Beloved Country* touches on many themes; some of these themes included forgiveness, love, unity, tolerance, and so on. The following is a theme card with a quote that highlights the themes of unity and love.

| Front | Back |
|---|---|
| Theme: Unity and Love | "I see only one hope for our country, and that is when white men and black men … desiring only the good of their country, come together to work for it … I have one great fear in my heart, that one day when they are turned to loving, they will find we are turned to hating." |

# Top Ten List

**Objectives:**

- To analyze a thematic topic from the story
- To improve comprehension of the work.

**Directions:**

- Think of a question about the work that would elicit discussion.
- Answer your question through composing a list of ten reasons why your answer is correct.

**Example:** In Shakespeare's tragedy *Hamlet*, there is a debate as to whether or not Hamlet's actions are because he has crossed the boarders of sanity or if he is just acting crazy. Here is a list of the top ten reasons why Hamlet is not off his rocker

## Why Hamlet is Sane
By Emma Beck

10. Hamlet warns his friends that he might act "a little strange" to cover up trying to revenge is father's murder (Act I, scene v, line 171).

9. Hamlet admits to his Mother that he has been "mad in craft" (Act III, scene iv, line 143).

8. When asked why she thinks Hamlet might be acting strangely, Gertrude's first responds that it might be because of her hasty marriage after her husband's death—not that her son is "crazy". (Act II, scene ii, line 56).

7. Hamlet's insults sting because they are true (Act II, scene ii, line 177).

6. Although Polonius insists that Hamlet is mad, he begins to wonder if there is method in his madness (Act II, scene ii, line 204).

5. Hamlet grieves for Ophelia's death (Act V, scene i, line 255).

4. Claudius senses that Hamlet is too aware of his guilt (Act III, scene i, line 189).

3. Hamlet shows remorse for accidentally killing Polonius; thus, demonstrating a conscience (Act IV, scene i, line 27).

2. Hamlet shows brilliantly his interpersonal intelligence throughout the whole play. The greatest example of this is when he is confronting his mother (Act III, scene iv, line 20).

1. Hamlet's ability to discern his inner-most thoughts and feelings show his sanity at the highest level (Act III, Scene i, line 57).

# Silent discussion

**Objectives:**

- To identify and analyze the themes of the work
- To discuss important literary aspects of the text
- To synthesize the purpose of the work
- To improve comprehension of the story

**Directions:**

- Make a list of themes, quotes or questions that would lead to discussion about the work.
- Write each of the topics on a piece of large butcher paper or poster board.
- WITHOUT TALKING, answer the questions using quotes and examples from the text.
- After you have had a chance to write a response on all of the topics, go back and respond to some of your peers' answers. "Silently discuss" the different topics with your peers.

**Example:** The following is a list of topics listed by themes used in a silent discussion on *The Crucible* by Arthur Miller.

**Intolerance:** Of what were people intolerant? Is intolerance still prevalent in our society today?

**Self-preservation:** How does this theme drive characters to do what they did? Do we ever see people doing things in our society today in order to save their own name?

**Fear:** How powerful is fear? What role did fear play in the story?

**Reputation:** Why was a person's name so important in the play? Is a person's reputation as important today?

**Ownership of land:** How does the ownership of land spur accusations in the play?

**Truth:** What is it? Who defines truth?

**Justice:** What is it? Were the Salem Witchcraft trials just? Do we have justice today?

*This activity is best when there are three or more people participating in the discussion. It is an ideal activity to do in a large group and is a unique way to give everyone an opportunity to share ideas in a safe environment.

# Vocabulary Ideas

When reading, it is important to take the time to look up unfamiliar words. As you do this, your comprehension of the story will increase and your vocabulary will improve. Try to incorporate the new words in your own writing. The following ideas will help you learn new vocabulary words.

# 15 Ideas to Learn Vocabulary

1. Write the definition in your own words.

2. Write a synonym and antonym for the word.

3. Look up the etymology of the word.

4. Draw a picture of your word.

5. Use the word in a sentence

6. What does your word rhyme with?

7. Make a connection with your word (this word reminds me of … )

8. Make flashcards with the word on one side and the definition on the other.

9. Write a poem using the vocabulary words.

10. Make a comic strip using the words.

11. Act out the word and have a partner guess the word.

12. Make a news report using your vocabulary words.  Film your report.

13. Have a spelling bee using your vocabulary words (see page 55).

14. Play Vocabingo with your vocabulary words (see pages 55 & 56 ).

15. Create a word map (see page 57).

# Spelling Bee

**Objectives:**

- To review the definitions of new vocabulary words
- To learn how to spell the new vocabulary words

**Directions:**

- Make a list of vocabulary words that you learned while reading a work.
- Look up the part of speech and definition of each of the words.
- Memorize the part of speech and definition of each of the words.
- Organize a spelling bee with other students or your family members.
- Designate a person to conduct the event.
- Compose a set of rules upon which all participants can agree.
- Set a date for competition and study!

**Option:** Buy prizes for the winners.

**Note:** Having a group competition is a great motivator to study and really learn a set of words.

# Vocabingo

**A fun way to review definitions of vocabulary words!**

Make a list of all of your vocabulary words and their definitions. Pick 24 of the vocabulary words and write them in the spaces on the *Vocabingo* board (one word per box). Pick a person to be the *caller*. The *caller* will randomly read the definitions of words. Make sure the caller keeps track of the words that have been used. As the definition of a word is read, mark off the word. The first person to get five words in a row wins!

| V B | O I | C N | A G | B O |
|---|---|---|---|---|
|  |  |  |  |  |
|  |  |  |  |  |
|  |  | Free |  |  |
|  |  |  |  |  |
|  |  |  |  |  |

# Word Map

**Create a word map by using a diagram like the one pictured below. The word is placed in the center box. Fill each oval surrounding the box with one of the following:**

- The definition in your own words
- A picture of the word
- A synonym
- An antonym
- A sentence with the word used correctly
- The Etymology of the word

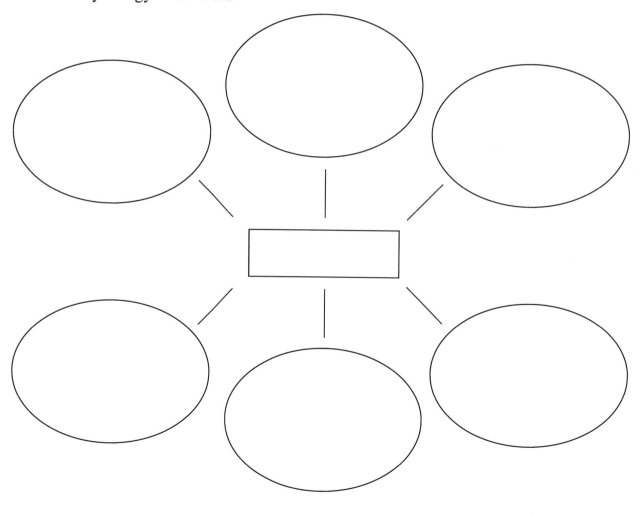

# Important Literary Terms defined

# Important Literary Terms defined

The following is a list of 100 important literary terms defined. These are words that are likely to be found on an AP English test in high school; they also serve as basic analysis for literature. It is important to understand these literary terms in order to comprehend the complexity of literature and appreciate the aesthetic qualities found therein.

Challenge yourself to become familiar with these words. Study a few of them everyday until you feel comfortable with the definitions. Then, have someone test your knowledge about each term by asking you questions. Or, create a trivia game to see how well you remember them. Ultimately, your goal should be to incorporate the different techniques and devices presented in this section into your own writing.

As you learn these terms, literature will become so much more than just an interesting story. You will find that classic literature is created with as much craftsmanship and technique as the most moving painting and the greatest architecture.

1.  **Allegory:** A story in which there are two levels of meaning; there is a coherent plot that can by analyzed, but there is also a second meaning in which *an extended metaphor is used to teach a lesson.* The author's purpose and the theme of the work can often be found in the second, deeper meaning (Murfin 9).

    **Example:** One of the most famous allegories in literature, "Allegory of the Cave," was written by the philosopher Plato in the fourth century. Plato used an extended metaphor—or an *allegory*—to illustrate the effects of education on the human soul.

    > And now, I said, let me show in a figure how far our nature is enlightened or unenlightened: Behold! human beings living in an underground cave, which has a mouth open towards the light and reaching all along the cave; here they have been from their childhood, and have their legs and necks chained so that they cannot move, and can only see before them, being prevented by the chains from turning round their head (from Book Seven of *The Republic).*

    Plato begins by telling the reader that he is going to use a figure, or a *metaphor* to teach "how far out nature is enlightened or unenlightened." Read the rest of the allegory to find out what happens to the men in the cave!

2. **Alliteration:** The repetition of consonant sounds at the beginning of words.

   **Example:** "While I *n*odded, *n*early *n*apping" from Edgar Allan Poe's *The Raven;* Jane Austen's *Pride* and *Prejudice* and *Sense* and *Sensibility.*

3. **Allusion:** A direct reference to something (a person, place, event, text or work of art) that is presumably known. The Bible is one of the most common works that is alluded to in literature. Pay attention to allusions in writing, as it is often a strategy used to make a point or show the author's beliefs.

   **Example:** In Alan Paton's novel, *Cry, the Beloved Country*, there are several Biblical allusions, from the names of the characters (Absalom, Stephen, John), to scriptures that are directly quoted. By incorporating Biblical references into his novel, one can see that Alan Paton is a religious man who feels that his beloved country will only be healed through principles found in the Bible (faith and love).

4. **Ambiguity**: Writing that is unclear in meaning and can therefore be interpreted in more than one way. Authors often purposefully use ambiguity in their writing to allow the reader to determine the meaning or the ending of the work.

   **Example:** The ending of Lois Lowry's novel, *The Giver*, can be interpreted in many ways because it is ambiguous. Some believe that Jonas and Gabriel die at the end, while others believe they find the old civilization from which their community broke apart. In her Newberry Medal acceptance speech, Lowry declared that there is no single "correct" ending because the reader's beliefs determine the book's meaning; thus, she purposefully wrote an ending that was unclear, or *ambiguous*, to allow the reader to determine the meaning.

5. **Anaphora**: A rhetorical device in which words or phrases are repeated at the beginning of neighboring clauses; anaphora is a type of *parallelism.* This repetition is typically included to put emphasis on a particular idea.

   **Example:** Harper Lee uses anaphora to show the reader that summer ultimately meant Dill (the nickname of a character) to the narrator. Words have been italicized for emphasis.

   > *Summer was* on the way; Jem and I awaited it with impatience. *Summer was* our best season: it was sleeping on the back screened porch in cots, or trying to sleep in the treehouse; *summer was* everything good to eat; it was a thousand colors in a parched landscape; but most of all, *summer was* Dill.

6. **Anecdote**: A short account of an interesting or entertaining incident. Think of anecdotes like a short interesting story. Telling an Anecdote is an effective device used to introduce the topic of an essay while getting the reader's attention.

   **Example:** If you were giving a speech on wilderness safety, a great way to capture the attention of the audience would be to start with an anecdote. The following anecdote happened to me   when I went camping in the Sawtooth Mountains once.

   > I was sleeping soundly when I was suddenly awakened by a loud, deep and grisly voice shouting "You get out of here you animal!" As I became more aware of my surroundings, I began to distinguish a heavy animal moving next to our tent-trailer. And then it hit me. There was a bear right next to us—trying to get into our coolers! My father-in-law had also heard the bear and had been the one who woke me up with his shouting.

   > After a few more minutes, the bear decided to move on and left us alone. Needless to say, we did not get much sleep the rest of the night. In the morning, we discovered teeth and claw marks all over the coolers. We sure learned our lesson—always lock up your food when you are camping—even if you think it is in an airtight container!

7. **Antagonist:** The opposing force; the thing or person that causes conflict for the protagonist or hero of a work. This can be remembered easily because the antagonist *antagonizes* the protagonist. Sometimes, the protagonist will be its own antagonist.

   **Example:** In Richard Connell's story, *The Most Dangerous Game*, General Zaroff *antagonizes* the character named Rainsford as Rainsford becomes hunted by the general.

8. **Antithesis**: A device that expresses the opposite idea, word theme, or character; a good synonym for antithesis is opposite. By studying a character's antithesis, you can better understand the character.

   **Example:** The vain queen in Disney's *Snow White and the Seven Dwarfs* is Snow White's antithesis. Snow White is sweet, kind, modest, happy, innocent and pure—while the queen is jealous, cruel, miserable, conniving and downright evil. Snow White becomes more sweet and innocent when *juxtaposed* against the villainous queen.

9.  **Aphorism**: A short, well-known saying; a tidbit of wisdom or a nugget of knowledge.

    **Example:** Morrie Schwartz from Mitch Albom's *Tuesdays with Morrie said,* "Learn how to die, and you learn how to live."

10. **Archetype:** A model or type after which things are patterned; a prototype.

    **Example:** Here are some common archetypes in literature: hero on a quest, villain, mother, outcast, star-crossed lovers, and savior.

11. **Aside:** A private remark that a character makes on stage to the audience, to another character, or to him/herself, but that is not heard by other characters on stage (think of this as a private "side" conversation).

    **Example:** In Act II, Scene II of *Romeo and Juliet,* Romeo is listening to Juliet speak and says to himself "Shall I hear more, so shall I speak at this?"

12. **Assonance:** The repetition of identical vowel sounds followed by different consonants in poetry; assonance is also known as vowel rhyming.

    **Example**: "p*ur*ple c*ur*tain" in Edgar Allan Poe's *The Raven.*

13. **Audience:** The group of people for whom the writing was intended; or the intended reader.

    **Example:** The intended audience for a children's story is children.

14. **Autobiography:** A form of nonfiction in which the writer tells his or her own life story.

    **Example:** *The Autobiography of Benjamin Franklin.*

15. **Ballad:** A literary balled is a narrative poem (a poem that tells a story) that has been composed with the intention of being sung. "Traditional" ballads, otherwise known as folk ballads, also tell a story and are passed down orally from one generation to generation; as a result, these traditional ballads tend to have many variations and the origins may be unknown. The term *ballad* has also been applied loosely to "slow-dance" love songs ("Lady in Red" by Chris De Burgh).

**Example:** Two traditional ballads that are fairly well-known are "Bonny Barbara Allen" and "Alouette." A famous literary balled is Samuel Taylor Coleridge's "The Rime of the Ancient Mariner."

16. **Blank Verse:** Poetry that is comprised of unrhymed lines all in the same meter; it is usually written in *iambic pentameter*.

    **Example:** The opening lines of Robert Frost's poem "Birches" are written in blank verse:

    > When I see birches bend to left and right
    > Across the lines of straighter darker trees,
    > I like to think some boy's been swinging them.
    > But swinging doesn't bend them down to stay
    > As ice-storms do …

17. **Biography:** A form of nonfiction in which the writer tells the life story of another person.

    **Example:** A biography about the life of Martin Luther King Jr. is called *I May Not Get There with You* by Michael Eric Dyson.

18. **Cacophony**: A mixture of unpleasant, harsh, or discordant sounds streamed together; it is the opposite of *euphony*. Cacophonous writing is short and hard to say.

    **Example**: Lewis Carroll's poem, "The Jabberwocky" is written cacophonously:

    > 'Twas brillig, and the slithy toves
    > Did gyre and gimble in the wabe;
    > All mimsy were the borogoves,
    > And the mome raths outgrabe …

19. **Catharsis:** This term means "purgation" or "purification" in Greek. It is the release (or cleansing) of unwanted emotions, particularly fear and pity, by the audience caused by exposure to a moving piece of art. Aristotle first introduced this term in *The Poetics* as the desired effect that a tragedy had on viewers. As the protagonist of a work endures challenges and trials, the audience also experiences all of the emotions of the main character and thus undergoes an emotional release.

**Example:** Sophocles's *Oedipus Rex* is a famous example of catharsis. The audience feels the emotions of Oedipus as he discovers that his wife, Jacosta, is actually his mother and that the stranger he killed on the road was his father.

20. **Character:** a figure that plays a part in the action of a literary work. The word *character* can also refer to a personality and even morality of a person in the story. Some characters are more developed than others (see *flat, round, dynamic and static characters*). *Characterization* is the process by which a writer makes a character seem real to the reader.

    **Example:** Jane Eyre is the main *character* (also known as the *protagonist*) in Charlotte Brontë's novel, *Jane Eyre*.

21. **Character Foil:** A character whose personality contrasts with, and thus highlights, the personality of another character; in other words, two characters that have opposite personalities.

    **Example:** Romeo and Mercutio could be considered character foils. Romeo reacts to situations emotionally and is quite serious by nature, and Mercutio likes to make jokes (his sole purpose is to add comic relief).

22. **Climax:** The high point of the plot—usually the part of the story with the most emotion (see *plot*).

    **Example:** In Disney's movie, *The Lion King*, the climax is when Simba returns with Nala to the Pride Land and battles Scar to become king. This is the highest point of emotion for the viewer; after the battle, the story begins to resolve.

23. **Colloquialism:** The use of language that portrays the speech patterns and vocabulary used by a particular people; in other words, an author captures the voice of a people by spelling things the   way people speak and sound, rather than writing correctly. See *dialect*.

    **Example:** Mark Twain's *The Adventures of Huckleberry Finn* captures the voice of many different *dialects* of people living in the south during the 1800's.

24. **Comic Relief:** The use of humor to lighten the mood of a serious or tragic story.

    **Example:** Shakespeare uses the gravedigger scene in *Hamlet* and the *character* of Mercutio in *Romeo and Juliet*, as comic relief.

25. **Conflict:** A dramatic struggle. Conflict forms the basis for plot and drives the story forward. There are several types of conflict in literature: *man vs. man; man vs. self; man vs. nature; man vs. society; and man vs. technology.* See *plot.*

    **Example:** Jack London's short story, "To Build a Fire" is about a man trying to survive alone in the wilderness. The main conflict, or *struggle*, in the story is his ability to survive in the harsh winter conditions. This conflict would be classified as *man vs. nature.*

26. **Connotation:** An associated meaning of a word in addition to its *denotation,* or literal meaning. The *connotation* of a word can vary in different contexts and even from person to person. The connotation of a word affects a writer's choice in words.

    **Example:** When writing "The Raven," Edgar Allen Poe considered using a parrot repeat the work "Nevermore." This, however, would have changed the entire *tone* and *mood* of the poem, as a parrot is a colorful bird with a positive *connotation*, and a raven has a darker, more dismal association.

27. **Consonance:** The repetition of final consonant sounds following *different* vowel sounds.

    **Example:** The lines from Wilfred Owen's poem "Arms and the Boy" provide an example of *consonance*:

    > Let the boy try along this bayonet bla*de*
    > How cold steel is, and keen with hunger of bloo*d*;
    > Blue with all malice, like the madman's fla*sh*;
    > And thinly drawn with famishing for fle*sh*.

28. **Couplet:** Two consecutive lines of poetry that usually rhyme and have the same meter.

    **Example**: The following couplet comes from the last two lines of Shakespeare's famous sonnet 18.

    > So long as men can breathe or eyes can see,
    > So long lives this and this give life to thee.

29. **Denotation:** The primary definition of a word, or the meaning found in the

dictionary ("d" for "dictionary definition"); the literal meaning of a word.

**Example:** The denotation of the word *home* means "a structure in which one dwells"; however, the connotation of *home* could be "a place of refuge."

30. **Device:** Tools writers use to accomplish a specific effect in writing.

**Example:** *Imagery, metaphors, symbolism, allusions*, etc.

31. **Dialect:** Dialect can refer to the method used by Greek philosophers to discuss conflicting ideas. In literature, however, it is the form of language spoken by people in a particular area or region (writing the way a person speaks).

**Example:** Mark Twain was one of the first writers to use different dialects in his writing. The following excerpt form *The Adventures of Huckleberry Finn* shows two different southern dialects (Jim is a runaway slave and Huck is a young, uneducated boy). Note how differently Jim talks.

> "We's safe, Huck, we's safe! Jump up and crack yo' heels. Dat's de good ole Cairo at las'. I jis knows it" (Jim).
> "I'll take the canoe and go see, Jim, it mightn't be, you know." (Huck)

32. **Dialogue:** A conversation between two or more *characters* in a literary work. Dialogue is used to develop the plot of the story and reveal information about characters. A new paragraph usually indicates a change of speaker.

**Example:** In Charles Dickens *A Christmas Carol*, three ghosts appear to the character Scrooge. The first ghost takes Scrooge quite by surprise. The following conversation is recorded as *dialogue* and moves the plot forward:

> "You don't believe in me," observed the Ghost.
> "I don't," said Scrooge.
> "What evidence would you have or my reality beyond that or your own senses?"
> "I don't know," said Scrooge.
> "Why do you doubt your senses?"
> "Because," said Scrooge, "a little thing affects them. A slight disorder of the stomach makes them cheats … "

33. **Diction:** An author's choice of words in writing. The two components that make up diction are vocabulary (choice of words) and *syntax*. To discuss an author's diction would be to consider the appropriateness of the words chosen, the vividness of the language, the way the words are phrased, and ultimately the effect of all of these choices. Others refer to diction as the way in which a person pronounces words.

    **Example:** Diction can be formal or informal, depending on the tone the author is trying to establish. Mary Shelly used very formal diction in her novel *Frankenstein*, while Zora Neale Hurston's choice of words is much less formal in *Their Eyes Were Watching God.* This is probably because Hurston tried to accurately capture the voice of the people in Florida, while Shelly's vocabulary reflects the more proper writing that was common of literature from the 1800's.

34. **Didactic:** Writing that has a moral lesson, sermon, or teaches something is *didactic.* Most didactic literature is written primarily to teach readers a specific lesson—whether moral, political or ethical. Many works may be considered to be didactic; however works that are mainly imaginative rather that purely instructive are not didactic.

    **Example:** Jonathon Edward's sermon "Sinners in the Hands of an Angry God" could be considered *didactic.* This was a sermon given to the early colonists in effort to call them to repentance.

35. **Drama:** A literary work that is written to be performed in front of an audience. Dramas are written in *dialogue* form and filled with stage directions to let the actors know how to move and act. Dramas are divided into sections called acts and smaller sections within the acts called scenes. Drama is one of the three major genres of literature.

    **Example:** *The Importance of Being Ernest* by Oscar Wilde was a very witty drama (play) written in the 1800's that highly criticized the Victorian society.

36. **Dramatic Irony:** *Dramatic irony* is when the audience knows something that the characters do not. Have you ever watched a movie and called out to an innocent character "Don't go there! It is dangerous!" But the character has no idea about the danger that is lurking around the corner? That is *dramatic irony*! Authors often use dramatic irony to create suspense.

**Example:** In Edgar Allen Poe's short story "The Cask of Amontillado," the reader learns that the narrator is seeking to get revenge on the character Fortunado. However, Fortunado believes that the narrator is taking him down to the catacombs to test a barrel of fine wine; thus, the audience knows that Fortunado is being lead to his death, but he does not.

37. **Dynamic character:** A character that undergoes an important change in the course of the story. Note that these changes are *within* the character, not just changes in circumstance. For example, a dynamic character will gain new insight or understanding throughout the story, or may have a change in values or ideals.

    **Example:** Ebenezer Scrooge is the quintessential dynamic character. Throughout the course of *A Christmas Carol*, Scrooge changes from a selfish, acrimonious man to a kind, generous and thoughtful person. Note that all these changes are internal.

38. **Epic:** A long narrative poem usually about a hero who undergoes a series of challenges and great achievements.

    **Example:** Homer's *Iliad* and *Odyssey* are examples of *epic* poems.

39. **Epic simile:** An epic simile, also known as a Homeric simile, is an elaborate comparison of unlike subjects. The simile is often several lines long and is typically used in epic poetry to intensify the heroic stature of the subject.

    **Example:** The following *stanza* from Homer's *Odyssey* is an example of an *epic simile.* This simile (rather graphic) is when Odysseus and his men blind the Cyclops.
    > as a blacksmith plunges a glowing ax or adze
    > in an ice-cold bath and the metal screeches steam
    > and its temper hardens — that's the iron's strength
    > so the eye of the Cyclops sizzled round that stake!

40. **Epithet:** Any word or phrase applied to a person that describes a quality or characteristic of that person. Epithets are often derived by taking an adjective phrase and applying it to a noun to accentuate a characteristic.

    **Example:** "Richard the Lion-Hearted" is an epithet of Richard I; "man's best friend" is an epithet for "dog"; and "Tricky Dick" is an epithet for former president Richard Nixon.

41. **Epistrophe:** A rhetorical device in which words or phrases are repeated at the end of neighboring clauses (see *anaphora* and *parallelism*). The is a great rhetorical device used in writing and speeches to create emphasis on a certain idea.

    **Example:** Ralph Waldo Emerson once said, "What lies behind *us* and what lies before *us* are tiny compared to what lies within *us*."

42. **Essay:** A short literary composition written about a particular theme or subject. Good essays have a solid introduction with a thesis statement, a middle section (called the body), and a conclusion that ties all the points together. Essays are often classified into the following four categories:

    a.   **Expository:** An essay that gives information, exposes and discusses ideas, or explains a process.
    b.   **Argumentative:** An essay that proves valid ideas with reasoning while convincing the audience (through persuasion) to feel a certain way. This type of writing could also be considered a *persuasive* essay.
    c.   **Descriptive:** An essay that seeks to convey an impression about a person, place or event; in other words, it describes.
    d.   **Narrative:** An essay that tells a story.

43. **Etymology:** The study of word origins and how words have evolved into their current meanings and forms; the lineage of a word. Studying the origin of a word can bring new insight to the meaning of the word.

    **Example:** Diligence. From Dis—apart, and legere—to choose. The meaning is literally "to choose apart," or "To single out." As it passed through French it gained a connotation of love. Thus, to lovingly single out. To do something diligently is to accomplish each part of the task with care and love.

44. **Euphemism:** A word or phrase that is used in place of another because it is less offensive or direct; one might say that it is the politically correct way to say something (Nadler 57).

    **Example:** "Kick the bucket," and "bought the farm" are euphemisms for death.

45. **Euphony:** The word *euphony* is derived from the Greek roots meaning "good sound." Euphony is a pleasant spoken sound that is created by smooth consonants; euphony is the opposite of *cacophony.*

**Example:** John Keats poem "To Autumn" is filled with euphony as it is easy to read and pleasant to hear. Here are the first six lines of the poem.

> Seasons of mists and mellow fruitfulness,
> Close bosom-friend of the maturing sun;
> Conspiring with him how to lead and bless
> With fruit the vines that round the thatch-eves run;
> To bend with apples the moss'd cottage-trees,
> And fill all fruit and ripeness to the core

46. **Farce:** A type of comedy filled with several improbable situations and mix-ups, slapstick humor, and crude *dialogue.* Humor in a farce is outlandish and obvious.

    **Example:** Oscar Wild's play *The Importance of Being Earnest* could be considered a farce as Wilde makes fun of the elite English upper-class through his stereotypical characters and humor.

47. **Fiction:** *Prose* writing that tells an imagined story, or has imaginary characters and events; see *genre.*

    **Example:** E.B. White's children's story *Charlotte's Web* is a fictional piece of writing.

48. **Figure of speech:** A literary device that is used to associate or compare distinct things; writers often use figures of speech to create an image in the reader's mind by setting up comparisons between two seemingly unlike things.

    **Example:** Some common *figures of speech* used in literature are: *similes, metaphors, personification* and *symbolism.* James Hurst used a simile in the following passage from his short story, "The Scarlet Ibis." This simile creates a vivid image in the reader's mind while introducing one of the themes of the story: death. " … the oriole nest in the elm was untenanted and rocked back and forth like an empty cradle."

49. **Flashback:** A scene that interrupts the present action of a narrated work to depict an earlier event.

    **Example:** The majority of the movie *Forrest Gump* is a series of flashbacks, or memories of the main character Forrest. The audience learns about Forrest's life as he reminisces on a bus bench. (Note: Please consider ratings before viewing any form of media).

50. **Flat character:** A character that is not well developed and only has one dominate trait. Typical characteristics of flat characters include villains, nerds, body builders, or any other character that can be stereotyped by a single characteristic. This is the opposite of a *round character* (or a well-developed character).

    **Example:** Mr. Collins, in Jane Austen's *Pride and Prejudice* is a flat character. He is a pompous, esoteric clergyman that has no other characteristics (which adds to his comedic effect).

51. **Foot:** The metrical unit by which a line of poetry is measured. There are five common types of feet in English poetry: *iamb, trochee, anapest, dactyl,* and *spondee.*

    e. *Iamb:* a foot with one unstressed syllable followed by a stressed syllable (as in the word "be-<u>FORE</u>"). (The stressed syllable is capitalized and underlined for emphasis; the syllables have been separated by dashes for clarity.)
    f. *Trochee:* a foot with a stressed syllable followed by an unstressed syllable (as in the word "<u>KIT</u>-ten").
    g. *Anapest:* a foot with two unstressed syllables followed by one stressed syllable (as in the phrase "on-the-<u>BEACH</u>").
    h. *Dactyl:* a foot with one strong stress followed by two unstressed syllables (as in the word "<u>CAN</u>-a-dal").
    i. *Spondee:* a foot with two strong stresses (as in the word "<u>BACK-PACK</u>").

    The type of foot that is most common in the poem will determine if the poem is described as *iambic, trochaic, anapestic,* and so on (Prentice Hall 953) .

    **Example:** Samuel Taylor Coleridge's poem "Metrical Feet—A Lesson for a Boy" exemplifies the five major forms of metrical feet.

52. **Foreshadowing:** The technique of giving clues about future events, actions, or revelations in a story. The use of foreshadowing keeps the reader speculating about what will happen next and creates suspense.

**Example:** On the way to the Capulet ball, Romeo tells his friends that he has a foreboding feeling about attending the dance.  In Act I scene iv, he said:

> I fear, too early; for my mind misgives
> Some consequence yet hanging in the stars
> Shall bitterly begin his fearful date
> With this night's revels and expire the term
> Of despised life, closed in my breast,
> By some vile forfeit of untimely death.

Through Romeo's speech, Shakespeare is foreshadowing that Romeo's life will be cut short because of what will happen at the ball.

53.  **Free verse:** A poem that does not have a regular rhythmical pattern, or *meter*.  Free verse also does not rhyme, usually contains irregular, short lines, and seeks to capture the rhythm of common speech.

   **Example:** Walt Whitman wrote many poems in free verse.  The following excerpt is from Whitman's "Leaves and Grass."

   > All truths wait in all things
   > They neither hasten their own delivery nor resist it,
   > They do not need the obstetric forceps of the surgeon.

54.  **Genre:** A category or type of literature that is classified based on the content, form and technique of the work.  The word comes from the French *genre* meaning "type" or "kind."

   **Example:** The three major genres of literature are *poetry, prose*, and *drama*.

55.  **Haiku:** A type of Japanese poetry that is three lines long.  The first and third lines of a haiku have five syllables; the second line has seven syllables.  Haiku poems seek to make a particular impression or evoke an emotion through creating images from nature.

   **Example:** Matsu Basho, a famous Japanese poet, wrote the following haiku.

   > An old silent pond
   > A frog jumps into the pond
   > splash!  Silence again.

56. **Hyperbole:** An extreme exaggeration used for emphasis.

    **Example:** I am so hungry I could eat a horse!

57. **Iambic pentameter**: A metrical foot that consists of two syllables—the first is unaccented and the second syllable is accented (or stressed). The iamb is the most common metrical foot in English poetry (see *foot* and *meter*).

    **Example:** Each foot (the unstressed, stressed syllable combination) in iambic pentameter sounds like this (the stressed syllables have been accented for emphasis):

    Goodbýe | Goodbýe | Goodbýe | Goodbýe | Goodbýe |

    The following line from Shakespeare's MacBeth is written in iambic pentameter (the stressed syllables have been accented for emphasis):

    Awáy | and móck | the tíme | with faír |est shów

58. **Idiom:** A phrase or an expression whose meaning is different from the meaning of the individual words. Idioms vary from region to region and are unique to each language.

    **Example:** "It's raining cats and dogs." "I am in a pickle." "Spill the beans."

59. **Imagery:** Descriptive language in literature that is used to create word pictures for the reader. These images are created through the use of sensory detail (detail that tells reader what to see, smell, hear, feel).

    **Example:** "The Secret Life of Walter Mitty" by James Thurber employs imagery to help the reader experience Walter Mitty's dreams. One can easily hear and visualize the following passage because of the use of sensory detail: "The commander's voice was like thin ice breaking. He wore his full-dress uniform, with the heavily braided white cap pulled down rakishly over one cold gray eye."

60. **In media res:** A narrative technique in which an author begins a story by plunging into the middle of a crucial situation (or action scene) that is an important part of the plot. In other words, the author opens the story in the middle of the plot, rather than the beginning. The word comes from the Latin phrase meaning "into the middle of affairs".

**Example:** David McCullough's novel *John Adams* begins *in medias res* with a sketch of Adams as he rides to the First Continental Congress, and then narrates chronologically.

61. **Irony:** A contradiction or incongruity between what is expected to happen and what actually happens in a work. There are three types of irony in literature: *verbal irony, dramatic irony,* and situational irony. (See *verbal* and *dramatic irony* for definitions and examples.)

    **Example**: If a cardiologist had a heart attack while attending a cardiologist convention, it would be considered irony (situational), because one does not expect a heart doctor to have a heart attack (especially while attending such a convention); thus it is a contradiction of what is expected to happen. In Richard Connell's short story, "The Most Dangerous Game," Rainsford, a hunter, becomes hunted by the character, General Zaroff; thus, the hunter becomes the hunted.

62. **Juxtapose:** To put or place two things side by side in order to compare and contrast the differences and similarities. By juxtaposing two things, one is able to easily draw parallels and understand the differences between the two different things or ideas. This can is a very useful tactic in comparing ideas in an essay.

    **Example:** When we juxtaposed our senior photographs with our parents', we could see that my brother has our mother's nose and I have our father's eyes.

63. **Metaphor:** A figure in speech that associates two unlike things together and compares them. Unlike a *simile,* a metaphor implies comparison <u>without</u> using the words *like* or *as.*

    **Example:** Our love is a tree; it grows bigger with time.

64. **Meter:** The rhythmical pattern of a poem; this pattern is determined by the number of beats in each line. To determine a poem's meter, take note of the syllabic pattern of each line (in other words, count the number of syllables in each line and see if there is a pattern). Lines in English poetry are described by the number of *feet* that they contain, as follows:

    j.    *Monometer:* poems written with one-foot lines
    k.    *Dimeter:* poems written with two-foot lines

l.  *Trimeter:* poems written with three-foot lines

m.  *Tetrameter:* poems written with four-foot lines

n.  *Pentameter:* poems written with five-foot lines

o.  *Hexameter:* poems written with six-foot lines

p.  *Heptameter:* verse written with seven-foot lines (Prentice Hall 953)

**Example:** "The Charge of the Light Brigade" by Alfred, Lord Tennyson is written in *dactylic* (see foot) *dimeter.*

65.  **Monologue:** A speech by one character in a play, story, or poem. In other words, it is a speech in which one character is monopolizing a conversation. Monologues are used by drama students to audition for a play.

**Example:** In Shakespeare's *Romeo and Juliet,* The Prince of Verona makes a long speech, or *monologue,* commanding the Montague and Capulet households to stop fighting.

66.  **Mood:** The atmosphere or feeling of a work. Often, a mood can be described by one word, such as dark, lighthearted, or despairing. The descriptive details found in the setting of a work are helpful in inferring the mood.

**Example:** The mood in Edgar Allen Poe's "The Raven" could be described as lonely or dark. This mood is created in the opening lines as the setting is established.

67.  **Moral:** A lesson that is taught through a literary work. A fable usually ends with a moral that is directly stated.

**Example:** Slow but steady wins the race is the moral to Aesop's fable "The Hare and the Tortoise."

68.  **Motif:** A recurrent image, word, phrase, object, idea or action that tends to unify the literary work is considered a *motif*; such motifs may be elaborated into a more general theme. When trying to identify a motif, look for situations, ideas, or images that are repeated throughout work.

**Example:** The colors green and white are repeatedly used in critical scenes in F. Scott Fitzgerald's *The Great Gatsby* and are considered to be motifs.

69. **Myth:** A fictional tale explaining the actions of gods or the causes of natural phenomena. Unlike legends, myths have little historical truth and involve supernatural elements in their explanations. It is interesting to note that every culture has its own collection of myths.

    **Example:** A famous Greek myth is the story of how Zeus became the ruler of the gods. According to myth, Cronus, Zeus's father, swallowed all of his children to prevent them from overthrowing him. Rhea tricked Cronus into thinking he was swallowing his son Zeus, when actually he swallowed a stone swaddled in blankets. Meanwhile, Zeus was secretly raised by mythical creatures; in the end, Zeus overthrew his father and became the ruler of the gods.

70. **Narrator:** The speaker or character through whom the author tells a story. The author's choice of narrator determines the point of view through which the story is told. See *point of view.*

    **Example:** The narrator in Harper Lee's *To Kill a Mockingbird* is a young, naïve girl name Jean Louise Finch (her nickname is Scout); because Lee chose to tell the story from the perspective of an innocent child, the reader hears the story from a less biased point of view.

71. **Non-fiction:** *Prose* writing that gives information about things, people, objects or events that are true.

    **Example:** *Seven Habits of Highly Effective People* by Stephen R. Covey is a classic non-fiction book about how to use time efficiently and how to life a fulfilling life.

72. **Onomatopoeia:** Words that imitate sound; knowing the etymology of this word bring insight to the definition. The word Onomatopoeia comes from two Greek words that when combined mean "to make a word imitating a sound."

    **Example:** Buzz, zip, pop.

73. **Oxymoron:** A combination of words with opposite meanings.

    **Example:** Jumbo shrimp.

74. **Parallel structure:** Phrasing two or more sentences the same way. An author uses parallel structure to place emphasis on an idea.

**Example:** Martin Luther King Jr.'s speech "I Have a Dream" is filled with parallel structure. The following passage from his speech exemplifies phrasing multiple phrases the same way (emphasis added):

This will be the day when all of God's children will be able to sing with new meaning "My country 'tis of thee, sweet land of liberty, of thee I sing. Land where my fathers died, land of the pilgrim's pride, from every mountainside *let freedom ring.*
And if America is to be a great nation this must become true. So *let freedom ring* from the prodigious hilltops of New Hampshire. *Let freedom ring* from the mighty mountains of New York. *Let freedom ring* from the heightening Alleghenies of Pennsylvania!

75. **Personification:** The act of attributing human traits and qualities to inanimate objects.

    **Example:** Stars wink from the sky.

76. **Plot:** The sequence of events in a story. A plot is based on a central *conflict*. It is the conflict that drives the events of the plot forward and captures the reader's attention (without a conflict, a story would be boring).

    a. **Exposition:** An exposition sets up the story, introduces the characters and gives background information (a good synonym for exposition is introduction). In addition, the exposition introduces the central conflict and often develops the themes of the story.
    b. **Inciting incident (also known as inciting force):** The event or character that triggers the conflict.
    c. **Rising Action:** A series of events that build from the conflict and leads to the climax.
    d. **Climax:** The high point of interest or suspense for the reader. The climax usually is the moment of highest emotion.
    e. **Falling Action:** The events after the climax that lead to the resolution of the story.
    f. **Resolution:** The end of the central conflict (when the conflict has been resolved). Another term that is used in place of *resolution* is *denouement,* a French term meaning "unraveling" or "unknotting." The resolution, or denouement, ties up the loose ends and concludes the story. In the case of a tragedy, a catastrophe may occur in place of a resolution. Gustav Freytag diagramed the parts of plot into a pyramid shape. Some critics have added a few elements to the pyramid.

**Example:** Here is an example of the parts of plot from *Romeo and Juliet.*

> **Exposition:** In the prologue, the reader learns that "star-crossed lovers" will experience "new mutiny" that springs from and "ancient grudge." The exposition continues during the first Act as it is revealed that Romeo is in love with Rosaline (a Capulet) and desires to go to the Capulet ball to see her (even though he is a Montague and forbidden to attend).
>
> **Inciting incident:** Romeo and Juliet meet and fall in love, only to discover that they are in love with their parents' enemy.
>
> **Rising Action:** Tybalt discovers Romeo attended the Capulet ball uninvited and vows to challenge him; meanwhile, Romeo and Juliet secretly wed.
>
> **Climax:** In a sword fight, Tybalt accidentally kills Mercutio (Romeo's best friend), and so Romeo then kills Tybalt out of revenge. Romeo is banished from Verona as punishment.
>
> **Falling Action:** Lord Capulet arranges a marriage between Juliet and Paris (even though she is already married to Romeo); Juliet decides to fake her own death. Romeo hears of Juliet's supposed death and vows to take his own life. Upon arriving at Juliet's tomb, Romeo encounters Paris mourning and kills him in a duel. Romeo takes the poison right before Juliet wakes up; Juliet, seeing her dead husband, stabs herself with a dagger.
>
> **Resolution:** As the prologue predicted, the grudge is ended with the death of Romeo and Juliet. The Capulets and Montagues declare that they will build statues of the other family's child in honor of their deaths and as a symbol of their newly found peace.

77. **Point of View:** The perspective from which a narrative is told. The choice of narrator determines the work's point of view. There are three perspectives from which a story can be told: *first, second* and *third.*

> **First person** is when a story is told from the point of view of a character. In this point of view, the story is depicted through the eyes of that character. The author will always use pronouns such as *I, me, my, mine, we,* or *us* in a story told from this perspective.
>
> **Second-person** is a story in which the author is directly speaking to the reader or addressing a familiar audience. This point of view is used when giving instructions because it tells the reader what to think, feel, or do. Writers will use the pronouns *you* and *your* when writing in second-person. This perspective is not used as often as the others.
>
> **Third-person** is a story told from the point of an outsider looking at the action; in other words, the narrator is not a character in the story. There are

two types of third person, *third-person omniscient,* in which the reader knows the thoughts and feelings of all characters, and *third person limited,* in which the reader only knows the thoughts from one character's perspective. The author will use the pronouns *he, she, his, hers, they,* and *theirs* when telling a story from the third-person.

**Example:** *The Trumpet of the Swan* by E.B. White is told from third person *omniscient* point of view.

78. **Poetry:** One of the three major literary *genres* (the others being *poetry,* and *drama).* There are many different ways in which a poem may be characterized. William Wordsworth, a famous poet, defined poetry as "the spontaneous overflow of powerful feelings." Dylan Thomas said "Poetry is what makes me laugh or cry or yawn, what makes my toenails twinkle, what makes me want to do this or that or nothing." Poetry can take many forms and is therefore difficult to define in one sentence. Poetry could be described as a subset of verse and can be lyrical at times. It is different from *prose* in that it is divided into *stanzas* instead of paragraphs, and the author can choose to capitalize the beginning of each line or not. Typically, poems are a series of short lines, and may or may not contain *meter* and/or *rhyme scheme.*

**Example:** One of the most famous of all poems is "Fire and Ice" by Robert Frost.

> Some say the world will end in fire,
> Some say in ice.
> From what I've tasted of desire
> I hold with those who favor fire.
> But if it had to perish twice,
> I think I know enough of hate
> To say that for destruction ice
> Is also great
> And would suffice.

79. **Prose:** One of the three major literary genres (the other being *poetry,* and *drama).* The word prose comes from the Latin "straightforward," and is ordinary writing (common writing). In other words, most works are *prose.* Generally, writing that is not considered poetry, drama, or lyrical is prose. Prose occurs in two forms: *fiction* and *nonfiction.*

**Example:** Any work that is not a poem, play or song could be considered prose. Prose could be a paragraph, an essay or an entire novel. An example of a novel written in prose is Laura Ingalls Wilder's *Little House in the Big Woods.*

80. **Protagonist:** The main character in a literary work who undergoes a conflict.

    **Example:** Harry Potter is the *protagonist* and Voldermort is the *antagonist* in the in the *Harry Potter* series by J.K. Rowling.

81. **Pun:** A play on words; a joke in which there are two or more meanings.

    **Example:** When a clock is hungry it goes back four seconds.

82. **Quatrain:** A poem (or a section of a poem) that is divided into four lines. Quatrains are usually written with a distinct meter and rhyme scheme.

    **Example:** William Blake wrote "The Tyger" in quatrains (four line *stanzas).* The following section is the first stanza of his poem.
    Tyger! Tyger! burning bright
    In the forests of the night,
    What immortal hand or eye
    Could frame thy fearful symmetry?

83. **Rhetoric:** The art of persuasion through writing and speaking. On a historical note, *rhetoric* was one of the seven major subjects (and more specifically, part of the trivium) studied in the medieval era. Aristotle stressed the importance of mastering the art of rhetoric as an essential tool of argumentation and oratory. He described three main forms of rhetoric, or three means of persuasion: Ethos (appeal based on the character or authority of the speaker), Logos (appeal based on logic or reason), and Pathos (an emotional appeal).

    **Example:** Lawyers are people that must master the art of rhetoric in order to win their cases. Many lawyers use logic (Logos) mixed with an emotional (Pathos) appeal to persuade the jury.

84. **Round character**: A well developed character. A round character is believable because he/she has the complexity of a real person. A round character is the opposite of a *flat character.*

**Example:** Raskolnikov is a complex character from Dostoyevsky's *Crime and Punishment*, as he has many faults but also learns to overcome them.

85. **Rhyme scheme:** A regular pattern of words that rhyme. The most common rhyme scheme is end rhyme (when the words at the end of the line rhyme). To figure out the rhyme scheme of a poem, look at the last word of each line and decide if it rhymes with any of the previous words; if it does, assign a lower case letter to each new rhyming sound (start with, the letter "a" and then move alphabetically).

    **Example:** William Wordsworth's poem "I Wandered Lonely as a Cloud" has a rhyme scheme that is easy to identify. The rhyme scheme in each *stanza* is *ababcc.* Here are the first six lines of the poem; the rhyme scheme has been marked (emphasis has been added to show the rhyme scheme).

    | | |
    |---|---|
    | I wandered lonely as a *cloud* | a |
    | That floats on high o'er vales and *hills* | b |
    | When all at once I saw a *crowd* | a |
    | A host, of golden *daffodils;* | b |
    | Besides the lake, beneath the *trees* | c |
    | Fluttering and dancing in the *breeze.* | c |

86. **Satire:** A work that ridicules something for constructive purposes; a form of attack on human follies or vices. A satire is usually written with a sarcastic or sardonic tone and its purpose it to comment or criticize a specific issue.

    **Example:** Jonathon Swift's "A Modest Proposal" is a classic example of satire. Swift wrote this piece to comment about the problems facing Ireland in the 1700's. He purposefully proposed outlandish solutions to the hunger and population problems in order bring exposure to these issues.

87. **Setting:** The environment in which a narrative takes place; it includes the time and place of the story. Time can include the historical period, but also the time of year and the time of day. The place may involve a specific geographic region, but it also may include a certain cultural environment. The setting plays a crucial role in developing the *mood* and tone of the work (a story that takes place on a dark December night in a forest would naturally have a scarier tone than one set in bright meadow in the middle of the day).

**Example:** Edgar Allen Poe's poem, "The Raven" is set in a student's study a little after midnight on a dreary December night. The tone is set in the opening lines of the poem as dark and lonely—all because of Poe's choice of setting.

88. **Simile:** A figure of speech in which a comparison is made between two things that uses the words *like* or *as*. Similes are very powerful because they help the reader visualize what the author is describing.

    **Example:** Louisa May Alcott used the following simile to describe a budding new relationship in her novel *Little Women*: "All sorts of pleasant things happened about that time, for the new friendship flourished like grass in spring."

89. **Soliloquy:** A long speech in which a character "thinks aloud" (alone) on stage to himself or herself. A soliloquy allows the audience to here a character's thoughts. A good way to remember soliloquy is that the character is "solo" on stage.

    **Example:** Hamlet's speech "To be or not to be" is a famous example of a soliloquy.

    > To be, or not to be--that is the question:
    > Whether 'tis nobler in the mind to suffer
    > The slings and arrows of outrageous fortune
    > Or to take arms against a sea of troubles
    > And by opposing end them …

90. **Sonnet:** The word sonnet comes from the Italian word "sonnetto," which means "little song." A sonnet is a lyric poem that almost always consists of fourteen-lines and contains a specific *rhyme scheme.* The Shakespearean sonnet, or the English sonnet, is the most famous of all sonnets. English sonnets are usually written in *iambic pentameter* and employ the following rhyme scheme: *abab cdcd efef gg.*

    **Example:**

    > Shall I compare thee to a summer's day?
    > Thou art more lovely and more temperate:
    > Rough winds do shake the darling buds of May,
    > And summer's lease hath all too short a date:

Sometime too hot the eye of heaven shines,
And often is his gold complexion dimm'd;
And every fair from fair sometime declines,
By chance or nature's changing course untrimm'd;
But thy eternal summer shall not fade
Nor lose possession of that fair thou owest;
Nor shall Death brag thou wander'st in his shade,
When in eternal lines to time thou growest:
So long as men can breathe or eyes can see,
So long lives this and this gives life to thee.

91. **Stanza:** A group of lines in poetry that are usually physically divided by a space or a blank line (think of a stanza like a paragraph in a poem). Stanzas are sometimes named according to the number of lines in which they are grouped.

> *Couplet:* two-line stanza
> *Tercet:* three-line stanza
> *Quatrain:* four-line stanza
> *Cinquain:* six-line stanza
> *Sestet:* six-line stanza
> *Heptastich:* seven-line stanza
> *Octave:* eight-line stanza

**Example:** A *haiku* is a poem that contains three lines, making it a single three-line stanza poem.

92. **Static character:** A character that does not undergo important change in the course of the story, remaining essentially the same at the end as he or she was at the beginning.

**Example:** All of the characters in Lois Lowry's *The Giver*, other than Jonas and The Giver (and potentially Gabriel) are static characters. They are static characters because they do not have the ability to feel, therefore, they do not have the ability to change.

93. **Symbol:** An object, person, or place that represents something beyond itself. Colors can also be symbolic in literature (red often symbolizes love or life; black symbolizes death or sorrow; green symbolizes growth and new life). Pay attention to symbols that are repeated throughout a work, as they usually are

clues that point to a theme.

**Example:** James Hurst's short story "The Scarlet Ibis" contains many symbols. The most obvious symbol is the ibis (an exotic bird), which represents the narrator's younger brother and also symbolizes death.

94. **Syntax:** The order of words in a sentence or line. An author's choice of how he groups a set of words affects the fluency of the line and the tone of the work. An author's syntax can also emphasize a certain word or meaning. Syntax is an important element of *diction.*

    **Example:** The first line in Robert Frost's poem "Stopping by Woods" is inverted. The normal order of a sentence is subject, verb, object, but Frost chose to change the order (object, verb, subject). He wrote: "Whose woods there are I think I know." Yoda, the master Jedi from Star Wars also spoke with an inverted syntax. One of his famous sayings is "Do or do not, there is no try." Note: these are just examples of inverted syntax which show how an author can choose to change the order of a sentence; as a result, such a change can affect the way a sentence sounds and flows.

95. **Theme:** The main idea or underlying meaning of a work. It is an idea that has been repeated throughout the work and is often the author's purpose in writing. In some works, a theme can be viewed as the moral or the point of the story. **Example:** A few themes in Victor Hugo's classic *Les Misérables* are love, compassion and forgiveness.

96. **Thesis:** A thesis statement is sentence or a series of sentences that presents an author's argument or purpose in a paper. A thesis statement essentially summaries the purpose of the essay and states what the author is trying to prove. It serves as a road map for the reader and directs the ideas of the rest of the work. When writing an essay, it is imperative to compose a thesis statement and make sure all evidence supports it.

    **Example:** If a person were given the writing prompt *"write a five-paragraph essay that illustrates the importance of forgiveness"*, they would need to compose a thesis that addressed the topic and set up the rest of the paper. A possible thesis would be: *Forgiving is important in order for one to maintain relationships, be happy, and ultimately be forgiven.* In the paper, the author would elaborate on the three points defined in the thesis statement.

97. **Tragedy:** A serious and somber drama that typically ends in death or disaster. All of Shakespeare's tragedies end in multiple deaths.

    **Example:** Classic examples of tragedies written by William Shakespeare are *King Lear, Hamlet, Othello, Romeo and Juliet, and Macbeth.*

98. **Transition:** Words used to connect ideas in between sentences. Well written essays include transitions that build a bridge between ideas.

    **Example:** Some common words or phrases are "in addition," "therefore," "furthermore," "another symbol used in the story," etc.

99. **Verbal Irony:** When a character says one thing but means something else.

    **Example:** in "The Cask of Amantillado," Montresor tells Fortunado that he is concerned for his health and does not want to take him underground to the catacombs to see the wine. In truth, he is hoping that Fortunado will go down with him so that Montresor can privately seek his revenge.

100. **Voice:** Voice is a word that is used to describe writing that sounds unique to a specific author. Writing that has great voice has a distinct style and unique personality. *Voice* is considered to be one of the traits of good writing.

    **Example:** Dave Berry, a former columnist for the *Miami Herald,* is known for his sardonic voice and creative wit.

# Notes

## Introduction

The quote by Abigail Adams was written in a letter to her husband in 1780.

The concept behind "doing something" with what you read is based on *Bloom's Taxonomy of Learning*, originally published in 1956. The theory states that comprehension and knowledge are the beginning stages of learning, while being able to put ideas together (synthesis), analyzing ideas and evaluating show the highest level of learning.

## Reading Strategies

The idea that strategies can be viewed as tools came from a college professor at BYU named Deborah Dean. For further information about approaching learning strategically (particularly writing strategically), see *Strategic Writing: The Writing Process and Beyond in the Secondary English Classroom* by Deborah Dean.

For further information about reading strategies, see *Strategic Reading* by Jeffrey D. Wilhelm.

## Activity Ideas

The student examples came from Eagle High School students in Jessica Collett's English classes and were used with permission.

The "Says/Does" concept came from a lecture given by Deborah Dean at BYU in 2004.

The Venn Diagram was introduced by John Venn in a paper entitled *On the Diagrammatic and Mechanical Representation of Propositions and Reasonings* in the *Philosophical Magazine and Journal of Science*.

## Important Literary Terms Defined

A great resource for definitions of literary terms is *The Bedford Glossary of Critical and Literary Terms* by Ross Murfin and Supryia M. Ray.

The list of literary terms came mostly from a series of lectures given by Rachel Roach, AP English teacher in 2001.

# Works Cited

Antinarella, Joe and Ken Salbu. *Tried and True: Lessons, Strategies, and Activities for Teaching Secondary English.* Portsmouth, NH: Heinemann, 2003.

Dean, Deborah. *Strategic Writing: the writing process and beyond in the secondary English classroom.* Urbana, IL: NCTE, 2006.

Domblewski, Carol, et al. "Literary Terms Handbook." *Literature: Timeless Voices, Timeless Themes.* Gold Ed. Englewood Cliffs, NJ: PTR Prentice Hall, 1999.

Murfin, Ross and Ray, Supryia, M. *The Bedford Glossary of Critical and Literary Terms.* Boston, MA: Bedford's/St. Martin's, 2003.

Nadler, Jay, Jordan Nadler and Justin Nadler. *Words you Should Know in High School.* Avon, MA: Adams Media, 2005.

Ogle, D. K-W-L: A Strategy for Comprehension and Summarization. *Journal of Reading* 30: 626-31. 1983.

**Reading and Writing Workshops**

More information at
www.learnwithmestore.com